Dust of Darkness

Book One
THE REIGN OF DARKNESS

By

Scarlet Hunter

DUST OF DARKNESS, BOOK ONE, THE
REIGN OF DARKNESS

BY

SCARLET HUNTER

Lucky Cl♣ver™ Publishing

Cordova, TN 38016

(The clover emblem/logo and the seal
containing name Lucky Clover is a
trademark of Lucky Cl♣ver™ Publishing)

Cover artist/illustration: VR

Editor: Leanore Elliot

Lucky Cl✹ ver™ Publishing

Warning: **This book may contain graphic sexual material and/or profanity and is not meant to be read by any person under the age of 18.**

Dedication

To all the book lovers out there. Thank you for allowing me to share my adventure with you.

PROLOGUE

*Beyond the depths of the universe,
unholy creatures breathed in and out,
fire and pain. Recognized and branded
by mortal humans as demons of the
underworld. Fiends of the fallen angel,
Lucifer and primarily known as The
Watchers to their prey. Taken from
their once mortal human life, and
possessed with a demon.*

*A new destiny to exist for centuries
with a lifetime tormenting those holy
and pure. Lucifer and his fiends sought
the most vulnerable of all races,
humans. To strip every bit of purity
their soul contained and corrupt it from
beliefs of right and good, with evil and
hate.*

*All would have been going
according to Lucifer's plan, if only for
one species; Fairies. A race neither
human nor spirit; yet beings who held*

one key element which kept the demons from spreading darkness across the realm of humankind—fairy dust.

CHAPTER ONE

"Hurry Raina, it's almost time!" a giggling child shouted while jumping up and down, clapping her small hands together with excitement. Her dazzling gaze glued on a shimmering circular-shaped magical portal floating a few feet above the ground. A rainbow of colors sparkled like glitter, shining high above the bright green blades of grass like an arched doorway.

Getting ready to leave for her assignment, Raina gracefully fluttered her wings stretching out behind her as she gazed over at the child sending her a warm smile. "Gwendolyn, you make me want to be young again. How I do envy the life of the progeny." Raina's grin widened as she bent down and kissed the top of the little girl's curly chestnut-covered head.

The progeny peered up with beaming eyes. "I wish I could go with you on this year's spring coloration," lamented, changing her smile to a disappointing frown while her fingers fidgeted with the bright pink lace of her dress.

Raina had been her mentor for five yearly seasons in Tulatopia, their fairyland.

A dreamland of fairies living far beyond the heavens, where darkness never ventured. A magical land of enchantment, where one would encounter sweet perfumes of everlasting flowers that never withered. Waters of emerald-green ran fluently down the mountain waterfalls. A vast array of birds of every breed flew amongst the land bestowing a telepathic communication between them and the fairies.

In addition to the diversity of birds, lived other varieties of God's animals existing throughout the magical kingdom. A utopia, humans would call such a place if discovered. A destiny ordained by mother-nature, ensuring their beauty and colors of life would spread across the planet during one particular season. The earth people called it, spring.

"Gwendolyn honey, I promise when you get a little bit older, I personally will take you on your first coloration."

Gwendolyn's eyes brightened and a grin spread across her dimpled cheeks.

Raina fluttered her wings and took flight toward the portal. Before she went through, she turned around. "And that will be the day you will get your first batch of fairy dust, to awaken the sleeping buds, trees and stalks amongst the earth's land, to millions of blooming flowers. When you witness the miracle as they stretch toward the sun, adding color and beauty to the world surrounding it, it will be a feeling you will never know until that day."

Gwendolyn burst with excitement, jumping up and down with anticipation for when she would get to go out and color the world.

Raina sent an encouraging smile back to her little friend, then flew through the portal. Her last thoughts as she passed through were of the evil spirits who also lurked on the other side. Those she purposely did not mention to the progeny, not yet. It wasn't all a bed of tulips.

The purest of evil known as, *The Watchers,* waited on the other side and over time, more and more of her kind were being captured and killed. The main reason Raina had yet to bring Gwendolyn over to that part of the world. *The Watchers* were after a supremacy only a fairy possessed, their mark of power. If taken, it could be used for the opposite of its purpose— *Darkness.*

CHAPTER TWO

In the hidden depths of a forest, Sarkis stood and waited. Leaning against an old pine tree, he glanced behind him to catch the tip of the sun rising in the east. Only a few minutes and it would be completely exposed from behind the creek's waterfall along a large tall boulder of rocks. Seeking the human hikers all morning, Sarkis was hungry, and not for just the simple pleasure of corrupting their minds. He hungered for souls to quench his burning thirst. The purer their soul, the more it appeased his inner demon. "Come on already, damn it," he growled, hearing the four humans approach.

"Hey Shelly, you wanna go skinny dippin'?" A male laughed, teasing one of the four victims. Walking alongside the others, the man swung trout he caught earlier from a line.

Sarkis inched behind the pine to shade his figure.

"Dream on, Roger," Shelly retorted. Their footsteps drew louder, drawing closer to their camp.

Sarkis clinched his fists. *Fucking, come on!* His eyes had already switched to scarlet-red, ready to attack. He could taste the extraction of their souls, entering his cavity at the same time their minds grew dreary and eventually void. At last, their lifeless bodies would fall heavily amongst the dormant forest, only to wait until the next prey came to feed on their rotting corpse.

"Nada, how about you, sweetness? You like to play in the water." The same male, Roger, teased the other female.

"No! She is with me. Damn it man, do you ever stop?" Another male cut in, wrapping his arm around Nada's neck.

She grinned and the two paused to kiss.

Humans. Sarkis rolled his eyes in disgust and with his hand, took a chunk out of the side of the tree without realizing it until the sound startled the humans.

They froze. Petrified looks spread across their faces while at the same time a female's piercing scream erupted into the sky.

"Oh, my God, Look! Ruuuuun!" Nada screamed and all four took off in a stampede toward the direction they'd just come from.

Disappearing out of sight, Sarkis knew they wouldn't return anytime soon. Furious, he glanced over his shoulder. He knew they hadn't seen him.

There, standing a few feet away, he found the ill-timed animal. Tossing the bark to the side, hearing it smack against a tree and crumble to pieces at the base of its trunk, he stalked the bear, his razor-sharp fangs fully extracted. "You came between me and my prey you fucking fur ball!" In a flash of movement, Sarkis whipped around the black bear and snapped its neck.

The huge mass of fuzz tumbled over dead. It didn't have a chance to make a sound.

Shouting curses into the woods, fuming with anger after slaughtering the bear, Sarkis turned to chase after the fleeing humans when he heard something coming from the direction of the creek. A loud splash like someone jumped into the pool of water. He hadn't sensed anyone else. Sarkis sprinted in the direction of the waterfall and stopped dead in his tracks. *Holy shit!*

Fluttering above the creek waters was a female. Flapping a massive pair of translucent wings, like a giant butterfly. The enormous set stretched out behind her in a wide array, even a second pair attached at the bottom flapped rapidly, desperately trying hard to catch up with the superior ones.

Not being able to remove his gaze from such magnificence, Sarkis watched as her wings emitted rainbow-colored dust.

When the magical elements floated toward the water, they disappeared.

Sarkis and the demon possessed within him gasped. *Fairy!*

CHAPTER THREE

Hovering over crystal clear waters, Raina breathed in the fresh pine-scented air, capturing nature's welcome at her presence. She'd arrived early morning on the human's planet and by the way the dew tickled her nose, she knew the night's dampness still lingered in the air. She caught a glimpse of her shadow dancing up and down on a rock behind her and giggled in amusement. Then suddenly, something made her turn quickly and scan the bare woods around her.

A sense she wasn't alone caused her pointed ears to stand at full attention, seeking out any threat. Cautiously, she continued to scan and came across a doe grazing off in the distance. Smiling, she nodded to the deer and it leapt off deep into the forest, two fawns close on its trail. Turning her attention back to her assignment, the only sound she picked up was the rushing of the waterfall behind her.

Gliding through the air, graciously over the creek, Raina came to rest on land, and scanned her watchful gaze across the woods. When her bare feet hit the earth, her wings vanished. Standing, she appeared nothing more than human to the naked eye. She shook her head, allowing her long golden locks of hair to revitalize after her travels disheveled it. Assessing her apparel, she snickered at her choice of clothing for the day's mission. A light-colored pair of jeans hugged perfectly to her lean lower frame. Her reason for choosing the article of clothing stemmed from the different shades of pink crystals shaped in a butterfly pattern on its back pockets. She loved human fashion. To complement her pair of jeans, she chose a hot pink tube-top, allowing her wings to extend freely at will.

Although, fairies never wore shoes in Tulatopia, Raina played with the humans' latest trends. From patent leather pink Prada's which although loving the many different shades of pink they came in, she couldn't get past the uncomfortable toe-scrunching leather.

Plus, she always wondered how humans could cover the beauty of painted toes. Inclining her head, she snorted at her electric-pink toes wiggling back at her. *How could anyone hide such cuteness?* The last few years, she even discovered sandals and many different varieties of flip-flops. She flaunted a pair in hot-pink for a while, yet realized how much she missed the soft blades of grass beneath her feet, so she threw them all out and went barefoot from then on out.

Walking through the forest, Raina gazed around at all the lifeless trees as she strolled past them. Dead patches of grass covered with dried leaves and branches for as far as the eye could see crunched underneath her bare feet as she walked. The hibernation of winter surely left its mark. *Well, it's time to wakey, wakey.* Fingering a pink crystal pendant dangling from her neckline, she lowered her eyelids and then reached her arms above her head. Her set of wings reappeared behind her and slowly she rose off the ground. Slightly bending her legs at the knees, she opened her eyes and from her fingertips, a swirl of pink, purple, blue, and yellow fairy dust soared and twirled around the trees, a whirlwind of magic.

Next, she targeted her attention to the dull flat ground. Fluttering a few feet above its soil, another enchanted sprinkle of miracle-dust brushed over its sleeping state. Instantly, spouts of green blades poked and ascended from the earth. Amongst the areas of the newly spawned bright green grasslands upshot an array of tulips in shades of purple, yellow, and Raina's favorite, a mixture of red and white blooms followed by buttercups and daffodils. Her affectionate smile grew, as did the beauty around her.

Turning her attention back to the trees, her multihued glittering magic twisted around each branch and tree trunk like a lighted Christmas garland. She grinned hugely while watching tiny buds begin popping up by the millions from bare branches. Raina marveled at the splendor of life being created. Crabapples, cherry trees, and dogwoods stirred after being in a cheerless dormant slumber for months. Nothing could top the exhilaration of bringing life to the world...nothing.

CHAPTER FOUR

Sarkis beheld a stunning female, the likes of which he'd never seen. Even his demon agreed.

Long blonde hair flowed well past her ass. When the lovely creature turned around, a breeze carelessly blew through her strands of hair brushing kisses across her flawless almond-complexion face.

He wondered if Mother-nature's spring winds no doubt sent warnings of his arrival. He'd heard rumors of nature talking to fairies, yet he did not know for sure. Never seeing a fairy up close until now, he watched her float above the waters by the waterfall and strangely, she stood admiring her feet. *What the hell was that about?* A strange breed they were. However, captured by her beauty, it suddenly struck him; his species hunted and killed one as lovely as she. *How could they?* The possessed demon inside him intercepted. *Their fairy dust, fuck-stick!* Yes, he knew this, but he still wondered if they were all this exquisite? How could one kill such a vision?

Keeping at a distance, forgetting all about his hunger for the hikers, Sarkis avidly watched the fairy leap into the air, tossing fairy-dust around the trees and covering the earth. Witnessing the powers the fairy dust truly bequeathed; the gift of life. No wonder his master craved such means. The fairies used it to create, bringing light and life to everything around it.

His kind, instead of distributing life, they took it. Extensively proving why fairies had to be exterminated, so his kind could control and rule the world in darkness. Fairies were the only thing standing in their way. If the creatures no longer existed...the world would remain dead and lifeless. Never to be reborn, thus one by one, the demons could consume and control the souls of all humans. Guaranteeing the goodness of mankind to dwindle and then their master, Lucifer would take over the world; finally consuming it in darkness and evil.

With the realization, he would have the chance of adding to the number of the extinction to this race, Sarkis somehow couldn't find it in himself to harm her—*Not her.*

Trying to eliminate the distance keeping him from admiring her magnificence, he inched closer. Little by little, he closed in, picking up on another heart-stealing feature. With her back to him, he marveled at the way her clothing outlined the curves of her body, making him swallow hard and the bulge in his jeans grew. Trailing up from her slender legs, his fangs extracted when they landed on her perfectly pink-glittering, melon curved ass. Sarkis' heart rate increased the more his gaze traveled upward, having to adjust himself more than once from staring at her backside.

Then the beauty spun around and he thought his cock would burst through his pants while gazing upon her vivacious mouth-watering breasts perking against a thin layer of pink fabric. The lack of material tantalized him as it hid her breasts. The rest of her upper body was stark-naked. *Why did she cover the most exquisite part of her attributes?*

Hell, screw the idea of killing her, his new mission was how fast he could get that top off and replace it with his mouth and hands. The moment the idea of his lips sucking on her nipples made his shaft harden even more and his balls tighten. Apparently, they were undeniably onboard. The thought had him almost falling on his knees in pain. Palming a thick tree trunk, he leaned his massive frame against it and tried to regain himself, but things suddenly changed for the worse. Lost in the fantasy, a twig snapped underneath his heavy boot.

As a result, the fairy became aware of his presence.

Putting aside his inner cravings, he decided it was time to introduce himself.

Overjoyed by the beginning of the season's coloration, Raina's senses abruptly stopped her from continuing. She wasn't alone. Quickly descending, landing on earth, her wings retracted and she searched for danger. She heard nothing, saw nothing. The woods were quiet, too quiet. Not one chirping bird could be heard. Remaining still, she concentrated and expanded her search when a voice behind her broke the silence.

"Aw, what do we have here?"

She didn't need to turn around. Raina smelled him too late but knew instantly. *A Watcher.* Gradually turning to meet the demon's face, ready to attack, when their eyes met, an electric shock burst through her body. Demons were evil and supposed to be grotesque, weren't they? Surprisingly, her skin blushed from his striking masculinity radiating from every inch of his build. Heart thumping, rising along with her libido, Raina suddenly found her mouth parched. Clearing her throat, trying to find any saliva to swallow, she couldn't take her gaze off him. *He is the enemy, Raina...nothing more!*

When Sarkis snuck up behind the fairy, every muscle in his body tensed when her deep sapphire-blue eyes gazed back at him. Yes, this female, even though a fairy, was resplendent. Again, the hidden member inside his jeans jerked and he bit his tongue to hold back the orgasm threatening to surface because of her beauty.

Sarkis, needing to adjust himself cleared his throat again and seconds later, the fairy did the same. Is she mocking him? He hoped the female didn't notice, even though he never offered his hand in greeting, his cock sure did. *Pull yourself together. You're supposed to suck her blood not her sex, you shit!* His demon always shared his opinion at the perfect moments. "Do not fear me," Sarkis said inching closer.

"And why do you think I would believe one of, 'The Watchers?' " she replied firmly.

She is not afraid of me. Brave.

"Don't think I don't know why you're here. But I warn you now. You will never get what you seek." The fairy fumed, crossing her arms over her succulent breasts.

Damn it, don't do that. "What makes you think I'm after something?"

"You under estimate us demon, we are more than you think."

Well, fuck...now she really started to intrigue him. He could kill her in one flash of movement, yet she stood her ground and he admired her valor, her courageousness. Hell, it damn well turned him on. Sarkis crossed his arms over his chest and started pacing in front of her. "Tell me...since you know me so well, what is it you think I'm after?" Expecting another cryptic remark, he heard a burst of laughter and peered up to find her fluttering above his head instead. Instantly, a blast of fairy-dust hit him smack-dab in the center of his face.

CHAPTER FIVE

Floating gracefully above the demon, Raina let out another ear-splitting laugh as she watched him remain in place, frozen. Demons always underestimated fairies, they had for centuries. It tickled her how this one in particular thought he could get the best of her. Planting her feet on the earth's soil, she progressed forward.

Although he couldn't move, he retained all functions mentally.

Stopping, allowing only inches to separate them, her heart jumped. Raina's tongue ran along her lower lip, and she bit down, pondering the idea of what he would taste like. Despite that, she realized to reach his lips would require her to use her wings or stand on her tiptoes to even come close to his inviting mouth. Just the idea excited her.

However, catching the demon's fuming crimson eyes glaring back at her broke Raina from her day dream. The slenderness of her body stood at a disappointing five foot nine to his six foot seven godly build. The demon male engulfed her with his presence, yet she managed to fight back as if she stood equal in height.

"Aw, are *we* angry?" she sniggered, knowing he couldn't speak. Tapping her chin, she decided to have a little fun. Raina raised her hand and a colorful rainbow of dust sprang from her fingertips brushing gently across the demon's hardened face. "There now, you can speak. Although what you have to say will make no difference."She then waited, pacing around him in a circle.

"Do with me what you will," the demon finally spoke, "but once the others of my kind sense you, they will not be as kind as I have been. For your own good...leave."

Why would he, one of the evilest of races allow her to leave before other demons found her? *He is toying with you*. Well, two can play at that game. Lividly, she whipped around and locked her gaze with his, her hands forcefully cuffed at the sides of her hips. "And just what makes you think you've been kind to me?" Raina snorted. "I and I alone am the reason you have been unsuccessful in killing me. AND might I add, in keeping you from stealing my power. I'm *no* fool." She paused and then burst into a fit of laughter. "Wait! Could it be...maybe you don't want your race to see I captured you?"

Waiting for an answer, she couldn't help but skim her eyes over his body. Now that he stood immobile, she had the opportunity to really take him in.

Wearing a similar pair of colored jeans, he, however, filled them out differently. His thighs were triple the size of hers, connecting to a lean waistline. A white shirt halfway open as a breeze took advantage and lifted the material, due to a few missing buttons. Exposing a mass of tanned rippled abs and bare skin covering his taut muscles. The white linen blew wider, exposing the butterfly muscles forming on his back.

She eagerly yearned to touch all those muscles and threw her hands behind her back to keep her delicate fingers from meeting his wave of strength. They wanted desperately to trail up to his rock hard pecks before fingering the outline of his v-shaped muscular back muscles. Raina's eyes widened at his immense physique. Not able to look away, she grew angry when the wind ceased, closing the peep show. Quickly coming back to reality, she raised her eyes to his face. Her knees weakened and a rush of heat exploded from her core. Why didn't she notice his features before? There seemed to be more to him than just darkness.

Although his hair, dark and long as death itself, hung loosely along the sides of his neatly manicured goatee, if she looked closer she could sense there was something more to this demon. It even amused her to see a diamond stud in one of his ears.

When she landed her gaze on his piercing crimson eyes, she didn't realize she took a step back. *Were his eyes always that deathly shade of red?* She heard demons who grew angry, their pupil's and retina's changed to an evil red no one has ever seen before. Strangely enough, those stories were all too true. Unfortunately, she'd only find him in this state. They were after all...enemies. *Wonder what color they were under different circumstances?*

Catching her off guard, a pulsing pool of wetness rushed out from her center and her breasts perked, urgently requesting attention from this demon. Raina blushed. This never happened and surely not with—yet he did turn her on. *Hello! Fairyland to Raina?* Demons didn't have the capability of entering the minds of the fairies like they did humans, so he couldn't be planting those visions.

She put her back to him while realizing she was utterly and truthfully attracted to him. She enjoyed how he seemed to get more frustrated each time she stood up to his reprimands, yet when he first approached her, he never made one move to harm her, did he? *What to do with him now?*

Squeezing her eyes shut, taking in a deep breath, she spun around and glared at his narrowed eyes. "Why so quiet demon? Afraid others will see you were captured by the likes of me?" Trying not to let him see her own weakness of arousal, she stood her ground.

His eyes trailed from staring at the ground, then along her body and up to her face, burning straight through her.

Raina gritted her teeth, fighting back the urge of throwing her arms around his neck and kissing the hell out of him just to fulfill her curiosity. She knew if they parted alive, she'd never see him again.

"You are a brave one I must admit. Tell me, are you this brave when not using your power?" He smirked.

"Your trickery will not work on me, fiend. I know all your ploys. You cannot out smart me." She was enjoying this.

"Then, if you don't believe I mean you no harm, remove your hold and find out."

Raina's heart increased its already intense rhythm. She couldn't trust him, she shouldn't. But, before she came to her senses, she sprayed another dose of fairy-dust releasing the spell taking a few steps backward. She wanted to see, to test him. One wrong move, and a wave of her hand, the spell would be reinstated.

The demon ran his thick fingers through his long strands of hair and cleared his throat. "Thank you." He bowed.

She didn't like the gesture in his bow. His kind didn't submit to hers. Yet, she couldn't help tilting her head to the side, admiring the way his body moved.

"May I?" He indicated he wanted to move closer.

Raina should have said no, but couldn't find her voice. Not admitting to herself of how she wanted him closer. *Have you lost your mind?* She swallowed hard when he slowly approached and hoped he couldn't hear the rapid thumping her heart made against her chest.

One foot after the other, he closed the distance between them until they were mere inches apart. He raised his hand.

She didn't move away. When it came in contact with the side of her face, she foolishly found herself leaning toward his embrace, accepting it.

"Your touch feels good upon my skin," he spoke softly moving his thumb back and forth along her cheek. With his other hand, he reached forward and played with the ends of her hair. He leaned closer.

Raina lost all inhibitions and met him as his mouth covered hers. *This is a trap you fool.* His kiss was gentle at first. When she did not pull away he deepened it, their tongues fighting to gain ownership, neither wanting to submit. Dueling out a battle of passion, she sucked and seized hold of his tongue in hunger. Maybe it was the rush of kissing the enemy.

Her hands finally able to pursue her fantasy while freely running up his hard abdominal muscles, and breaking along his sides, then up along his powerfully built back. Her fingers slid upward, gripping the tops of his shoulders and pulling him closer, deepening the kiss even more. "What is your name, tell me," she panted, breaking the kiss enough to speak.

"Sarkis," he answered taking her by the waist and lifting her off the ground, wrapping her legs around his waist, pulling her closer to him before taking her mouth again.

Raina instantly felt his erection against her core. *Oh,* yes. *Sarkis.* She liked the way his name sounded in her mind and the affect she unmistakably had on him.

He broke their kiss. "And yours?" he asked and smothered her lips again.

Dare she give in to the enemy? Those were the last words she thought before whispering into his mouth while yielding, "Raina."

CHAPTER SIX

Raina. Her name running over in his mind made Sarkis crave more than just this fairy's touch. He yearned to explore every fraction of her body. His demon remained silent. If he objected to the desires flowing through his mind, surely the demon would express his protest. Yet, no influence of his objection lured Sarkis to continue.

The way she dominated their kiss and the softness her touch on his skin as her palms moved up along his abdomen, sent shivers up his spine. He never knew simple contact between flesh, could stir such a reaction. Lost in the passion of the moment, his fingers landed at the button fly of Raina's jeans.

In result of the encounter, she pulled back and jumped from his arms.

The moment Sarkis' fingers began to unbutton her jeans, the reality of how he was the enemy made Raina flee his hold. Panting, she leapt into the air, landing on the ground several yards away. Two fingers rested upon her swollen lips. The demon tasted as sinful as she imagined and even standing far from him now, she craved more.

Only seconds passed since she vanished from his side, when he appeared right in front of her. His hand instantly reached for her face, the longing desire in his eyes burning back at her.

Raina, scared to allow herself to give in, abruptly shot into the air once again, this time she soared through the woods, straight toward the portal leading back home.

Again, the demon pursued her.

The minute she reached the waterfall, she landed, while his immense frame stood hot and sexy behind her. She could feel his intense breath brush against the tips of her shoulders.

Swallowing hard, she wanted to turn around, but couldn't.

When she took a step forward, a hand lightly seized hold of her upper arm. *Do not submit to him!* With everything she had, she flipped around, causing his grip to release from her arm and she took to the air. Her wings fluttered behind her with great speed as they mimicked her anger and the eccentric wild lust she felt toward him. She glided through the air, drawing closer to the waterfall.

The spring winds produced mist from the water and it swept across her back while she hovered over the center of the creek. Turning to face Sarkis, she tried to keep her expression firm. "Like I said, *demon*, you underestimate us fairies!" Before giving him a chance to speak, Raina flew through the portal.

With her arms crossed and head down, Raina moved slowly along the rainbow-colored stone brick path leading home. Once she passed through, she destroyed the portal behind her, so Sarkis wouldn't be able to follow. The sweet aroma of fresh flowers filled the air around her from the garden grounds which embodied the life of Tulatopia. Again, evidence of how her and the demon's world were total opposites. So, why did he occupy her every thought? Trying to convince herself to block all thoughts of him, an image of a small child skipping toward her made her smile at the much needed distraction.

"You're back! You're back," Gwendolyn sang as she drew nearer.

With a warm grin, Raina greeted her little friend. "Gwendolyn, how nice to see you, sweetie."

Gwendolyn's innocent face glowed with delight. When she reached Raina, she threw her arms around her as she always did.

Raina embraced her. "Well, it's good to see you, too."

While walking side by side, heading in the direction of the fortress, Gwendolyn took Raina's hand in hers. She swung their arms back and forth as they strolled. "Please take me with you when you go back next time...please?"

The question made Sarkis reenter her mind. Just the thought of him harming Gwendolyn...

"Raina, what's wrong?" Gwendolyn asked.

The tugging of Raina's arm snapped her back and she realized she was frozen in place. "Oh, I—uh, I'm sorry sweetie. I guess I'm a little tired."

"Well, you never answered me. Can I...*pleeease*?" she begged

"Gwendolyn I promise you, the next spring coloration, I'll take you with me, how's that?" Raina knew by the look on her little friend's face, she didn't like her reply.

Then, she turned her small curly-haired head at Raina and smiled. "Okay," she answered squeezing Raina's hand and they continued their journey toward the fortress.

Neither said another word the rest of the way.

"For the love of..." Raina yanked the sheets away from her body and kicked

the bottom of her heels against her mattress. Frustrated by the fact she couldn't fall asleep. Imagery of Sarkis corrupted any hope of getting rest. No matter how much she fought it, the demon enraptured her; more so than she could comprehend. She tried everything to fight against it. But realized she didn't want to. *Why couldn't it work between them?* After she withdrew her power from him in the woods, he made no attempt to harm her. A real monster wouldn't have kissed or touched her the way he did, right?

Getting out of bed, she stomped over and sat at her vanity. Its center covered in hot pink faux fur where all her perfumes, lipsticks and other assortment of cosmetics were assembled in a perfect row. Raina picked up her brush and began combing her long strands of golden hair. Staring back at her reflection, a fantasy of Sarkis' face appeared as if he stood behind her. A smile lit his face while staring back at her. She knew she wanted to see him again. It was a big risk, but one she was willing to take. She just hoped he wanted her as much as she wanted him.

Knowing dawn would soon begin to break on the other side, Raina left the fortress and headed toward the garden grounds. With great stealth, she opened another portal before anyone woke. Taking a deep breath, she rose off the bright green blades of grass and soared through the portal. The moment she appeared on the other side, she glided across the still creek waters and landed on the soft ground.

The morning sounds of birds chirping in the back-ground mixed with the rushing of the water behind her echoing. The pounding of her heart beat heavy inside her chest. She hoped she'd see him again. Then like a gift from heaven, she turned to head in the direction she first crossed paths with him.

Stopping dead in her tracks, her breath caught. Sitting on a wall of stones at the far end of the creek's embankment, sat Sarkis. The expression on his face, reflecting his temptation, erased her fears.

He stood and disappeared, only to reappear right in front of her.

Jeopardizing it all, she gave in to all matters of self-control. Raina didn't know if it was love, but she sure as hell was going to find out.

In unison, they both jumped forward and embraced.

"Damn it woman, don't ever do that to me again," she heard him say to her ear. Sarkis squeezed her tight against his chest, then pulled back and captured her mouth with his and scooped her up into his arms, careful not to break their kiss. Carrying her, the demon took a few steps, and then knelt down, placing Raina upon an array of purple flowers. His hands swiftly lifted and removed her tube top, allowing her breasts to pop free.

When his mouth came in contact with her ready and willing bosom, Raina surrendered. Heart and soul, she gave herself completely into the hands of the enemy.

CHAPTER SEVEN

What the hell are you doing? Sarkis thought while his mouth kissed and sucked over the fairy's breast, his hand caressing the other. Just like he imagined, they were perfect. *You cannot do this to her. She is good, you are evil.* Battling with himself mentally, he couldn't fight it.

When she disappeared in front of him the day before, all importance of his existence died. In result of her departure, the demon inside of him roared in pain. He made a vow to himself he would stay; never leave this spot until he saw her again. To show her, despite being her enemy, he could be more if she would only allow him to prove it to her. Yet, all night he waited...he did not rest, nor did he eat. Nothing would draw him away until he saw her again.

Then, moments ago, when the outline of her petite body appeared in the middle of the creek, his heart as well as his cock jumped. Sarkis wasn't going to lose her again; he intended to make damn sure of that. The touch of her skin, the way she tasted might be addictive. Like a drug, he wanted more until he overdosed on pure pleasure. Discovering someone this extraordinary existed and now that he did, he and his demon desired more. Sarkis realized with Raina, he'd forgotten his evil side.

If life could be like this, he wanted it and would do whatever it took to keep it—to keep her. For the first time, he wanted to worship something by choice; to worship her. All his past lovers were nothing but to appease him and his demon. This time, he wanted to please her in every way and he wouldn't leave an area untouched or unsatisfied. Even his demon hummed from the source of pleasure.

With his hands resting above her head, knees positioned at her waist, Sarkis treasured her reaction as she wiggled and moaned at the way the cool breeze tickled her skin from his wet kisses. Pulling his body slightly back, he placed his fingers on the button fly of her jeans and waited for her approval. When she smiled and nodded, he stripped the denim along with her lace panties from her body with one quick pull. Sarkis took the time to admire her body. "You're beautiful," he whispered. In that moment, his heart broke free from its black darkened shell of evil and hate, when she gazed into his eyes and smiled.

"They're green," she giggled.

"What?"

"Your eyes." Her smile widened. "They are as green and wild as four-leaf clovers."

Sarkis cleared his throat, flabbergasted. "It—It must be you, for I cannot recall any shade other than the redness of evil. I haven't seen their true color since being human centuries ago. You have brought out the good in me, Raina. It is the power you have over me."

"But, I didn't use my power—"

Placing two fingers upon her lips, he cut her off, "No, it is not your magical powers my beauty, but the power from within which can only be willingly given. The way you give yourself to me, unconditionally. You have surpassed the fear of who I truly am. You have even managed to tame my inner demon. In centuries, I never thought to see such a day." This fairy moved him in so many ways.

In the next instant, she proved it to him, as her hand came behind his neck and pushed him closer toward her, sealing their mouths in an enduring kiss.

The softness of her lips tasting of sweet cherries ignited a lustful desire making him explore deeper. With her, he let loose of everything he held back before. Craving this woman would only bring havoc, yet damn it—he couldn't fight it. Sarkis gave in, even his demon purred and submitted, yearning to embrace this new side.

His mouth inched away from her lips and lightly landed a kiss over each eye, and then moved, placing another on her forehead. Sending her a winsome smile, he made a trail down to her cheek, then along the sides of her neck. Kiss after kiss, he traced the length of her soft delicate skin. When she raised her hands and gently stroked his muscled back with her nails, he growled, and in chorus, she moaned into his ear from each of his pleasurable pecks. In seconds, the rest of his clothing was removed from his body.

The moment his aching erection poked against her inner thigh, a dominating growl erupted from deep within his chest. His stomach muscles clinched when she groaned at the contact. Sarkis bit the inside of his cheek trying to hold back from taking her. *Is she a virgin?* Oh, of all that is unholy, what if he hurt her?

"I need you—oh, Sarkis. Please," she begged as if in pain, I can't stand it anymore, I'm —I'm going to die if you don't..."

At her words, his demon took over, hissing inside Sarkis' mind. He couldn't bear to deny and leave her in pain for one second. Leaning back, he trailed his hand down the center of her breasts making her back arch up from the ground from the electric connection between them. Still on his knees, he lifted one of her legs and starting at the inside of her knee, laid a trail of kisses along her delicate skin, only stopping right before he reached her sweet spot. Sarkis inserted three fingers one by one, teasing and taunting until they were thrusting in and out, his thumb rubbing at her nub.

Raina screamed in ecstasy, twirling her fingers around and yanking at the

new blades of grass and flowers next to
her in unison with his probing fingers.
Her head moving back and forth, then
almost reaching her zenith, she cried
out, "Oh, for the love of fireflies! No, no,
no—Stop!"

Sarkis stopped abruptly and stared
at her in panic.

She quickly reacted. "No, no, no—
don't stop!"

He couldn't help but laugh and
continued. Yet, this time, he covered her
juicy folds with his mouth and moaned.
Now he knew the depths of heaven.
Devouring her sweet cherry nectar, his
cock stiffened and he couldn't get
enough as she came for him while
calling out his name like he was a god.
Hell, he felt like one. Sarkis took her
over the top and he then pulled back. He
grinned as he watched the fulfillment on
her beautiful face.

Taking his cock in his hand, he
positioned it at her core and when only
the tip of his shaft entered her, he
cursed. He wouldn't be able to do this
without exploding instantly. Squeezing
his eyes shut, letting his head fall
forward, he willed his cock to hold on a
little bit longer. Tightening his ass
muscles, he moved his pelvis onward

until his cock filled her completely. He paused for a second, panting.

Hearing Raina moan and feeling her tighten her inner walls around his cock was all it took. Sarkis roared like a lion on its prey. His inner demon hummed and he pounded into her with rapid thrusts; in and out, he drove his shaft in powerful plunges of need.

Hearing her cry out for more, compelled him to go even faster. The driving force of their slapping flesh against flesh rang out into the wilderness. Sarkis' balls constricted, ready to release fireworks. His abdominal muscles jerked and volcanic heat shot up along his shaft when she contracted against him in rapid spasms.

When Raina rocketed up and her breasts smacked against his own hardened and aroused teats, he lost it. She tightly seized his upper arms and cried her release triggering his own. Grasping her waist, he pulled her closer against his body. There wasn't a part of them not touching. He bellowed, shooting hot seed inside her as she covered him with her own warm sweet juices.

After they were both spent, Raina fell back onto the patch of purple flowers and a break of sunlight peeked through clouds shining a sparkling glow around her.

Joining her, Sarkis cupped their bodies together. Lying behind her, he softly placed kiss after kiss against a pair of hot-pink wings outlined in black at the center of her back. He'd never noticed them before, yet hadn't thought to look. He smiled and persisted with his kissing.

How could there be any other who could make him feel the way she did? In his years of existence, he never felt like he did now. Never came close. Yet, here they lay, a fairy locked in his arms, his prey trusting him not to harm her.

How did he deserve such compassion and faith from one so lovely?

Sarkis turned Raina around to face him and he traced the side of her face with his fingertip. Her eyes closed, her breathing still heavy, yet the racing of her heart calmed and soothed him. With words at the tip of his tongue, a voice off in the distance triggered both of them to rise in alarm. He knew the voice all too well. His temperament changed like the wind. "Get dressed, NOW!" he barked.

CHAPTER EIGHT

Stalking through the woods, pissed and on brink of losing control, Roderick hunted for his comrade. The day before, Sarkis claimed he needed to hunt and would return in a couple hours time, yet he didn't. Even the night passed without word from him. When someone didn't follow through, it infuriated him to no end. *Where the fuck are you?* Stomping through the forest, the sun peaked at its mid-day annoyance. Loathing to venture in the daytime, all he despised stirred in the brightness of the sun's exposing light.

The warmth of the sun's waves of heat annoyed him just as much as the species he was destined to kill. Too bad, he couldn't put an end to it as well. Darkness couldn't come soon enough. The more he traveled through the woods, the more his anger rose.

Lifting a cigarette to his lips, he pulled a silver Zippo skull lighter from his pocket and flipped the top open using his thumb. Flicking the flame to life, the eyes in the skull beamed red. He grinned every time he lit the fucker. He angled the lighter, tilting his head, and lit the tobacco rolled paper, sucking in the nicotine. His demon howled as the drug ran through his body. Flipping the top sealing the flame, he placed it into the back pocket of his jeans.

Jerking his head to the right, his senses caught an all too familiar scent. *Sarkis—and...?*
"Well...well...well...lookie what we have here," Roderick smirked with the cig between his lips. Taking in a long drag, he flicked the cigarette to the side and took off in a flat out run. Sprinting through the forest, he dodged trees and branches until he stopped where the scenery eccentrically changed from browns and burnt yellows of winter to electric greens and bright colors.

Fairy...
Roderick kicked at the sickening onset of green grass and purple flowers encircling an area his heightened sight picked up to be about a half a mile radius. His upper lip raised in a snarl

when he caught the flowery scents. "Fucking fairies!" he muttered under his breath. What pissed him off even more, Sarkis' scent was mixed in with the honey and lavender poisoned fumes.

"Where are you?" he barked. "I can smell your honeysuckle ass, you traitor!"

For centuries, he and Sarkis had been like brothers, the only two to outlive the wrath of their master Lucifer, thriving through the darkness and evil, together. Lucifer appointed them on his most important of tasks because the demons possessed within them always surpassed their ruthless and heartless acts.

Nevertheless, in the past few years, Roderick tried to ignore the awareness to Sarkis' distance and calmness in temperament during their latest missions. Not sure of the cause to this variation of his evil nature and why his demon did not surpass him. Then ever since, he always lurked in the shadows keeping a sharp eye on Sarkis, and reporting to Lucifer any signs leading to his treachery. This confirmed his suspicions.

The air reeked of the nearby fairy and...sex. Roderick growled with disgust. "Come now Sarkis, you know you can't hide from me. I'll find you and the fairy you're hiding." With a feverish evil laugh he continued, "I can smell her...and can't wait to sink my fangs into her flesh, having the pleasure of sucking the life out of her. You know my friend; it is not polite to keep her all to yourself. We are supposed to be friends after all. What is mine is yours and vice versa."

Gritting his teeth, Sarkis' fangs exploded from his mouth at Roderick's words. Clinching his fists he knew after today, either he or Roderick wouldn't leave the forest alive. "Get behind the tree and stay there. Do as I say. Do not move or speak a word," Sarkis ordered not looking back, hoping Raina would obey his command.

Roderick was powerful and would be hard to defeat. He'd never fought him before and didn't know if he would be successful this day. Yet, a strange energy ran through his veins. Was it the protective bond he felt for the female? Hell, he didn't know. Only one thing registered and mattered. Roderick wouldn't lay one finger on his woman. His old friend was near. He could smell the nicotine reeking from his pores, even from where he stood.

"Come on now, Sarkis. Hand her over and I'll forget to mention this to Lucifer."

Sarkis growled. His blood boiled, knowing Roderick's lies all too well. "Leave now Roderick and I will not have to kill you." Keeping his figure hidden behind a tree, he peeked around the bark and observed the form of his comrade coming into view. Looking over his shoulder, he didn't see her but knew Raina stood behind one of the pines about fifteen feet away. "Tsk. Tsk. Tsk...How you always like to play games. You know, I've never been patient with your schemes, Sarkis. They bore me."

His attention switched back to Roderick. "Then leave!"

"Aww." Roderick rubbed his hands together and laughed. "You seem a little on edge. Can it be you are hiding this fairy? Now why would you do that, I wonder?" The demon tapped his chin and headed toward Sarkis' direction.

The moment he approached, Sarkis growled and stepped into view. Only a dozen or so tall trees stood between them. *There was no way in hell Roderick would get any closer to Raina.* He roared in anger at about the same time Roderick took hold of something behind a nearby tree.

A loud squeal erupted, filling the silent woods when he jerked a small child by her curly chestnut hair and tugged her out into the open. A little girl with a look of utter and complete terror plastered across her face dangled from his hold.

The moment the child's cry pierced through the woods, the sound of Raina's wail followed.

Crouching down ready to pounce, Sarkis lowered his chin, his gaze never breaking from Roderick's glare. "Release her!" he yelled.

"It seems we have two fairies...how lovely. I hear the young are even tastier. I'm thrilled to finally find out if this is true." Roderick scoffed at the same time his head sloped down and his fangs reached for the girl's neck.

CHAPTER NINE

Watching the demon snatch something from behind a tree and then Gwendolyn's small frame coming into view, caught Raina by complete surprise.

Snatching her abruptly, he lugged Gwendolyn to a more open wooded area of the forest. Her baby-soft bare feet dragged behind her as a result of his forceful and heartless behavior to their kind. Gwendolyn released another scream when he slammed her small feeble body against him. She peered up at him and burst into sobs as his demonic fangs leaned in for the kill.

"Let. Her. Go!" Raina demanded while running toward them. Making sure, she put distance between her and Sarkis. As much as she hated it, she needed to save Gwendolyn and he would only stop her from advancing. "Take me, but don't harm her. She doesn't have what you seek. I DO!"

The demon violently threw Gwendolyn across the woodland and stalked toward her.

Raina's breath caught, seeing both Gwendolyn's fragile body being tossed, hitting hard against a bed of blood-red tulips, and at the now advancing demon.

"Noooo!" Gwendolyn cried, her petite body still rocking in pain on the ground. "Don't hurt her, she is my friend."

"Gwendolyn, I need you to do something for me." Raina never took her eyes off the demon. "Run...No matter how much it hurts. Run toward the portal and once you've crossed, make sure it is destroyed."

Gwendolyn slowly got to her feet, wiping the streaming tears from her sad innocent brown eyes. "But—you won't be able to—?"

"Don't worry about me. Do as I say. NOW!"

Gwendolyn took off running, rushing in the direction of the safe-haven, taking Raina's last chance of returning to Tulatopia with her.

With Gwendolyn safely out of sight, Raina started to pace backward as the demon drew nearer. Trying her best to keep her balance after tripping a couple of times on debris, she increased her pace. She needed to turn around and run, but it would be even more dangerous to lose sight of the crazed monster closing in. The beat of her heart raced for survival. So much ran through her mind, it didn't even dawn on her to use her powers like an idiot. Frazzled from worry for Gwendolyn's safety, of being left behind on this realm and by the demon now drawing closer.

Panicked, she came to grips of how this could be the end.

If Gwendolyn reached the portal and made sure it was closed, she would be stranded on the human planet. Once their portal was closed from the other side, a fairy could not retrieve its opening. A tear slid down the side of her cheek at the thought. Then suddenly, her back bumped into something massive and it took hold of her upper arms. *Sarkis*—could she really trust him now that one of his own wanted her?

"I'll have her blood running through my veins and will be rewarded when I bring her power to our master," the monster stalking her promised.

Raina gasped and her hand instantly went to her neck, finally hating herself for not using her powers on the demon.

At the same time, Sarkis' grip on her arms eased, but he didn't remove his hold. "You will not have her, not now, not ever! Leave now, Roderick, and I will allow you to leave, alive."

"Sarkis...Sarkis. Our orders are to kill them, and you know this. Killing her makes one less fairy and gets us closer to our purpose. There is no other option!"

Raina closed her eyes and her fingertips began to glow...About to blast him with her powers.

Sarkis whispered, "No, I'll take care of him."

She stopped, yet remained on guard.

"You're wrong and there is another option." Sarkis growled.

Roderick flashed his fangs. The dullness of his black pupils expanded, the whites of his eyes burning with crimson.

Raina held her breath at the demon's spine-chilling image and looked behind her to see Sarkis' were the same just as he pulled her harder against his chest.

"I won't allow this. The only option is Lucifer's and she will die!" Roderick hissed.

"Then, you will have to kill me first," Sarkis retorted.

"You turn your back on your own, for the enemy? Lucifer will be interested to learn this."

"He's no longer my master. Now either you leave us, or prepare to die." Sarkis yanked Raina behind him. Instantly, claws grew from his fingertips as he crouched down in a fighting stance. "Run!" he yelled at her as he took off, heading for the demon already rushing to meet him.

Raina hesitated for fear of what would happen to Sarkis. Why, she didn't know, but when she turned and ran through the forest, thoughts of never seeing him again caused a sharp pain to shoot from her heart. She wasn't ready to leave him. *Shit! What did that mean?* How could this man, this demon have this kind of control over her? Coming to the waterfall, Raina scanned the area and found no portal, just as she feared.

Bittersweet emotions overcame her, knowing Gwendolyn returned safely to Tulatopia, yet she lamented the fact she never would. Raina collapsed on a wall of stone beside the creek realizing in time, her fairy powers would leave her body. She would then start the process of fading till her spirit left her and returned to the earth where she came from.

Thoughts of sorrow filled her heart thinking of how she would miss her family, Gwendolyn and—then Sarkis' face appeared in her mind. Finding herself starting to worry more for him than her own outcome, she stood abruptly and turned; facing back in the direction she'd run from.

He fought to save her, could she not do the same? Heeding the fact, Sarkis did not want her to use her powers, wanting to fight the demon himself, she didn't care. No one threatened to hurt her man! While still possessing powers, she got to her feet and lunged herself into the air, flying vigorously through the forest. If she must remain on earth, she was going to damn well fight for him; demon or not.

Getting closer, she couldn't see them, but heard the crude sounds of male's shouts and grunts. She swallowed hard and increased her speed. Reaching the two finally, they were both covered in blood. Sarkis being pinned down by the one he called Roderick. Just as his rival's razor-sharp claw lifted behind him ready to attack, Raina flew down kicking him forcefully with the bottoms of her feet. Sending him flying off Sarkis' body, he crashed and slid on his side hard against the ground. Raina grinned at the harsh hit of his landing.

At least until her pink pendant necklace sparkled from inside the palm of his bloody hand. Her hand immediately took hold of her neck. *My power!* Without her pendant, she had no power. Tragic enough she couldn't venture back to her homeland, now the demon held the only remains of her powers contained in her pendent.

"Well, what do *we* have here...Missing something, sweetheart?" Roderick said half-winded, wiggling his eyebrows. Swollen with pride, he jumped to his feet dangling the jewel from his fingers.

Sarkis expelled air from his lungs with a harsh noise while pushing off the ground and only managed to get onto one knee, still trying to catch his breath.

It was all or nothing. Raina had to get it back. With all the power she could muster, her wings expanded and flashed in a speed of light, snatching the pendent from Roderick's teasing grip and shot back into the air.

She couldn't cast spells without the pendent, but she sure as hell could fly. After all, she was a fairy. "You will harm him no more!" she hollered, pulling the necklace over her head and then fairy dust instantly emitted from the tips of her fingers.

The second the dust swirled around his body, the demon cried out in pain.

"For you are nothing more than fire and death, return from that of which you came." At her words, the demon's body burst into flames, rich black smoke and remains of his burning embers engulfed the sky like a twirling tornado. With her eyes closed, she summoned a mighty spring wind to blow, lifting the ashes and taking them off to what Raina hoped was the direction of hell. Descending to the ground in front of Sarkis, her wings retracted behind her back as she helped him get entirely to his feet.

Sarkis' shaking hands took her by the waist and bent over to kiss her when all of a sudden she collapsed. Sarkis barely caught her before her body hit the ground. Worry filled his eyes. His warm loving arms wrapped around her tighter as he held her in the bed of flowers she brought to life.

A tear slid down her cheek, she understood what was happening, and accepted her sacrifice. Fairies powers were not to be used for the death of others. If so, the dark shadows of death would reciprocate and take their life in return. Cupping the side of Sarkis' face, she whispered, "Do—not—worry. I-I-lov..." Raina's eyes closed and as she faded into darkness, she heard Sarkis release a roar into the daylight's shadow.

CHAPTER TEN

She'd returned to him—and she saved him. "Raina! Raina! Wake up—come back to me." Sarkis jerked and shook the shoulders of Raina's lifeless body. Leaning over her unresponsive frame, a teardrop fell, hitting her cheek and he dropped his forehead on her collarbone. His arms protectively wrapped around her. "I love you. Do you hear me woman, I love you! You cannot leave me, not when I just found you." Sarkis couldn't recall the last time he experienced this powerful of an emotion.

Ever since Lucifer found him and took all forms of his humanity centuries ago by cursing him with a demon, he'd never felt anything but evil and hatred. Yet, staring down at Raina, he toppled over her motionless body and for the first time—wept. Sobbing for hours, an apparition of light and warmth made Sarkis open his eyes and slowly draw back from Raina. Vision blurry from the flood of tears, he couldn't believe what he saw. Standing up and away with utter shock, as Raina's whole body glowed.

A rainbow of colors beamed out of her pores like godly rays shining on earth through the clouds after a storm. The shafts of light soared high and disappeared into the star infested sky.

He'd been mourning for hours and realized night surrounded him. The luminosity engulfed her so intensely, Sarkis could no longer see the outline of her frame. He needed to step back and shelter his eyes with his hands from the blinding flash of light. Then, as quickly as the beam of joy came, it descended and vanished. Sarkis blinked several times to adjust to the restored blackness. In the few seconds it took, he gazed across the bed of flowers and his heart shattered. Falling to his knees, he stared at nothing but a dim moonlit outline of the grass and flowers crushed by Raina's body—her body was gone.

With his head hanging low, Sarkis ran his fingers through his hair and walked through the forest. His whole world had ended. He'd lost the only one who gave him kindness and rekindled the inner humanity he thought he'd lost forever.

His heart beat for the first time after being dead and merciless for centuries. Living became a whole new outlook to him and as soon as he found it, it died along with the only one who signified its meaning. What would he do now? He couldn't go back to the life Lucifer expected from him. Just thinking of his master, bile rose from his throat and he cursed. His master didn't even know he'd been a factor in Roderick's death, or did he?

Lucifer had a way of knowing things.

His breathing turned to rapid pulls of oxygen. The demon inside raged with the loss of Raina. Reaching his breaking point of grief, his malevolent set of wings he'd previously concealed only in worry of frightening Raina expanded behind him. The expansion caused his shirt to rip from his enormous frame, and he watched the torn pieces of fabric fall at his feet. With his dark gifts, he could hide his massive traits from most. So, up until now he concealed them. A vastness of black feathers soared seven feet in length behind him.

Sarkis dropped to his knees once again. Bending forward, his claws dug into the earth and he roared her name into the dark empty wilderness. His life would forever be consumed with nothing but darkness without her, just like before he'd met her. Though now, there would be a different purpose of hate.

He would return to his master. With one intention; to destroy him, securing that the fairy race would never be harmed again, even if it cost him his life. "So. Let. It. Begin."

"I want those fucking flies burned alive...All. Of. Them!" Sarkis heard Lucifer rant and rave as he made his way into the demon's lair. Staying in his demon form, black as night wings flapped massively behind him and he stopped at the doorway.

Lucifer must have sensed Sarkis' presence because in a flash, from once standing across the room, he now had their noses and foreheads pressed firmly against one another. A frenzy of anger raged from his crimson eyes. "Where the fuck have you been?" he snarled.

"Roderick is dead."

"I take it you had something to do with this?" he bit out condemningly.

"I didn't kill him if that's what you're insinuating," Sarkis growled.

"Then who *is* responsible?" Lucifer backed away, his arms folded across his cold-hearted chest.

"Whom do you think? Those of whom you were cursing as I entered."

Lucifer arched an eyebrow. "And just how did you manage to get away might I ask?"

"I witnessed the fairy killing Roderick. When I went to attack, the fairy fell to the ground and disappeared. I came straight here to tell you." Sarkis bowed hiding his hate as he added, "...master." It took every mental and physical control he could conjure not to expose his emotions over losing Raina. He tried to keep the details short.

Replaying what happened in his mind as
it pulled at his dying heart.

"Were there more of them? Where
were you?" his master shouted.

"I know where to find them." Sarkis
kept to the point. His thoughts focused
only on the task. If his master wanted,
he could easily enter his mind. He then
would become aware of his influence. It
seemed he hadn't.

Lucifer pointed to a troop of demon
fiends. "You, come with me." Flashing
his fangs, he snarled back at Sarkis and
locked eyes for a mere second, his
demon intensely jerked. Pushing his
finger heavily against Sarkis' chest, he
expressed his warning, "Lead the way. If
there are more, they will die! And if this
is some kind of game, the ending will be
your life."

With his master's gaze still locked
on him, Sarkis suddenly forgot what he
was supposed to do. *What had just
happened?* He was going to—but the
snarling crack of a grin appearing on his
master's face had him nodding and then
walking behind him. All those fairies
would meet their death this time. Don't
be merciful...leave none alive. His
demon purred, *yes for all shall perish*

and we will consume the earth to darkness and despair.

Sarkis followed his master. To put an end once and for all to the fairies; those pests would find out what it was like to mess with the king of darkness and his ruthless fiends.

CHAPTER ELEVEN

A cool damp object pressed lightly against her brow produced a trickle of water to slide down her temple. The soothing article lifted, causing her to release a moan from the removal of its cooling comfort. "No—come—back," she hoarsely managed to get out.

"She's awake! She's awake!" a familiar voice sang.

Raina cracked her heavy eyelids and four faces slowly came into focus.

Her sisters, Peony, Magnolia, Jasmine, and Freesia looked down at her. Each of them slanting over her with smiles spread across their faces.

Raina coughed. "Where am I?"

Before her sisters could answer, a small head poked from in between two of them, chestnut curls swooshing back and forth and Gwendolyn immediately began jumping with glee. "They brought you back!" she cheered with excitement. Her smile faded and a small hand rested on her arm. "I was so scared," Gwendolyn said wiping away a tear with her other.

Raina tried lifting herself up and her sisters immediately joined in to help her. Propping her arms behind her for support, she glanced at each one of them. "How did you find me?"

Magnolia spoke first, "Gwendolyn rushed into the fortress and told us what happened. Freesia came for you." She smiled, her raven hair pulled back in a tight ponytail. For months, she grew out her short strands of hair ever since she chopped them off, trying to attract a male she had the hots for, then she learned he preferred girls with longer hair. She and her sisters took her aside many a time, trying to get it through her stubborn head about how men should love a woman for who she truly is. Never alter to fit what they wanted because it ruined the gift of their eternal beauty.

"Why? Why did you do it? You should have let me die," Raina stated sadly. "You all must know what I did and what my actions meant—How could you bring me back?" Four hands reached on both sides of her, resting on Raina's shoulders.

"We are bonded, sister. We could not allow you to pass into the colorless end. You are too important to us," one of her sisters uttered.

"As head of this family and queen of the fairies, it was my decision," her sister, Freesia interjected. She stood tall with rose-red hair, and unmistakably, the most beautiful of them. She spoke softly, yet sternness lingered in her voice, "Come, allow your sisters to help you. You need food and then you and I will converse."

"I—I don't know what to—?"

"You don't have to say anything, sister. Gather your strength and then we shall talk."

Raina smiled at her queen and dearest sister while at the same time her other siblings took her by the arms to help her from bed and onto her feet.

Jasmine and Peony stood at her left while Magnolia had her right. "Come on sis, let's get you a hot shower," Peony urged.

"I think we should take her to get some food, first. She needs to replenish her strength," Jasmine argued.

Raina grinned, glad to be home. "Actually, I would like to soak in a warm bath if you don't mind." She laughed sending Magnolia a wink. Her sisters were always at battle with one another. Never had she heard them agree on anything.

"Whatever you want," Magnolia muttered, giving Peony and Jasmine a glare.

Leaning her head back against a pink bath pillow, Raina relaxed in a soaker tub, an array of rainbow-colored bubbles surrounding her.

A light knock tapped on the bathroom door and her sister Freesia's voice came from behind the block of marble. "May I come in?"

Raina sat up, startled out of her deep thoughts, as water swished back and forth from the sudden movement. Ever since she awakened, she couldn't get Sarkis out of her mind.

"Yes...do come in, sister," she answered.

The door cracked farther open and Freesia peeked in before entering. Closing the door behind her, she placed a glass bowl full of cherries on a table next to the oval free-standing tub. Then she sat on the pink fur-covered stool in front of Raina's vanity. She rolled her eyes at her sister's choice of décor and crossed one leg over the other, tucking her hands in her lap. Freesia's manner always seemed elegant and regal. "I know you must be hungry, so I brought your favorite."

"Thank you." Raina took a cherry and popped it into her mouth. "Umm, I guess I was hungrier than I thought."

"You're welcome," She paused, then sighed. "Now, tell me what happened out there? I know you were in danger, yet I'm confused at what I witnessed when I arrived...What I can't figure out and hope is not true—were you aiding one of the enemy? When Gwendolyn came and told me what happened, I rushed to your aid. But what I saw wasn't at all what I expected."

Raina squared her shoulders, her hands gripping the sides of the tub, anger in her eyes. "Sarkis is NOT the enemy!" she shouted.

Freesia frowned. "Oh, Raina. I feared this was what you would say. You allowed one in, didn't you?"

"I—I love him. I won't hide my feelings. Freesia, he's not evil. I promise. He helped me against one of his own. He never tried to take my power. You have to believe me." Raina turned to stare at the bowl of cherries. "Don't you?"

"Yes, dear sister I do believe you. But, what you must realize is this alters everything. I saved you because of your mistake. You should have died out there for your actions." Freesia stood and paced the marble floor. "I can't lose you or any of my sisters." She stopped and glared at Raina. "Even for a demon." She resumed her pacing again, throwing her hands up in the air.

Raina couldn't say a word. Her sister was right, but she loved Sarkis and would have gladly given her life for him. When he made love to her, he opened up a whole new world to her and it damn sure felt better than anything she'd ever encountered.

Her sister sighed deeply. "Okay, here is what we are going to do. We have to finish the coloration of spring. It seems demons are going to make this difficult for us this year, so we must be ready. I'm taking Jasmine, Peony and Magnolia. You, my sister...will be staying in Tulatopia. Sorry, but that is an order."

Raina stood up in the tub, bubbles ran down her naked wet skin, "But, I have to—"

"No! If there is anything going on between you and this demon, you will only be a liability. Forgive me sister, but this is my final word on the subject. I've already broken one of our sacred bylaws while saving you from our enemy. I don't want to have to do it again. Your sisters and I will leave for earth tomorrow morning at sunrise." Without looking at Raina, she left the room. Halting at the entrance for a brief moment, she released another heavy sigh and stepped out.

CHAPTER TWELVE

The crackling snaps of wood mixed with the smell of burning leaves hummed in Sarkis' ears and burned his nostrils. It was magnificent. He started the fires and sported a hard on while watching the flames grow higher and higher into the night.

On the way to the forest, Lucifer demanded to know how Roderick failed to survive against the fairy.

For some reason, the last several hours were nothing but a blur to Sarkis and he couldn't understand why. It seemed the only thing he recalled when crossing paths with Roderick had been watching a fairy blast his comrade in the face with fairy dust, turning him to ash instantly.

Lucifer, shocked at this new discovery grew angrier. It disturbed him to learn they could now be killed with the simple power of fairy dust. "Those rodents are becoming more of a thorn in my side than ever before. Kill them. Kill them all!"

Earlier on, during their trek to the forest, Sarkis carried a bushel of Witch Hazel in his arms.

Lucifer gladly gloated at this find, as fairies were weakened by the flower.

Sarkis' evil smile widened. The black seeds produced a toxic fume making fairies unable to fly and restricted, only for a small amount of time, the use of their powers.

The dawn sky finally made her appearance. The effects of the last few hours of burning flames engulfed the sickening spring colors of woodland, now burnt down to nothing but black ash and scorched tree trunks. Marveling over his doing, Sarkis heard an all too familiar sound off in the distance, like water rushing from a stream. His heart fluttered. Did this sound mean something, or someone? On the other hand, he couldn't quite recall what. An image floated across his mind.

His master's voice rang from behind, "Fairies!" Snapping his attention away from the image, "Sarkis, get into position and do not fail me, boy!"

Sarkis folded his massive black wings against his back and took cover behind a smoky-charred tree. With the sun rising, it was going to make it difficult for them to hide their numbers and he hoped the heavy arrays of smoke still lingering would suffice. "Get ready!" he called to the fiends.

There were fiends positioned all around the open woodland. Those fairies had no chance if they revealed themselves now. Better yet, each and every one of the fiends, including Sarkis and his master held in their hand the one thing needed to entrap them—Witch Hazel.

"Damn, Peony don't push." Jasmine shoved her sister back.

"Ya know, there's a flower I want you to get familiar with, sis. It's called the Pussy Willow!" Peony retorted.

Jasmine rolled her eyes. "Very funny, but I know demons are here, I can sense them. Am I the only one concerned here?"

Freesia held up her hand. "Silence you two. If they didn't know we're here, they sure as hell do now."

Jasmine punched Peony on the shoulder and whispered, "Pansy!"

Peony pointed her finger in her sister's face and mouthed off some choice words before Magnolia smacked them both on the back of their heads. "Shhh!"

Walking through the forest, they fell silent, stopping in unison when their eyes caught far off in the distance the only thing worse than their enemy.

Fire.

"Oh, no—Freesia! What are we going to do?" Magnolia wept. "The trees, the wildlife?"

"I'll tell you exactly what we are going to do, end this...Now!" Freesia announced and marched forward. Leading her sisters, Freesia's ears rang and her heart stitched from the pain she felt at the sight of the scorched trees and plants. The blackened grisly sight before her made her want to crawl on all fours and weep. Save for the fact, she could sense the enemy remained close. Too close for comfort. "They are hiding. Be on alert," she whispered, warning her sisters,

Then all at once, a ball of fire shot out from behind a tree and hit the ground inches from Freesia's bare feet, instantly flaring, the blaze casting a ring of fire around her and her sisters. Entrapping them.

The instant the ring sealed itself, a figure loomed and moved forward. "Aw, so we finally meet."

Freesia could make out only a small part of the figure dressed in black as dawn slowly took her time reaching over the horizon. When he drew closer, she could see the male's arms were crossed over his chest. Long shoulder-length slick hair outlined a face of pure evil. He halted his steps just outside the flames and the side of his mouth lifted in a snarl. "So, glad to finally meet you, and you brought friends, how nice."

"Don't think the burning of the forest will stop us, demon!" Freesia bellowed. "We will finish spring's coloration."

Roaring in laughter, he smirked. "Please, call me Lucifer. And I must say, for a fairy, your kind does have courage. A real waste if you ask me, for it has no real purpose, flies that you are."

Freesia gritted her teeth and her fingertips began to glow. Being queen, she held great power and was the most feared of their kind. The hands of her sisters took hold of her shoulders to increase her power. Just as she was about to cast a spell, another demon emerged, carrying something in his arms and tossed it over the fumes of the flames.

All four of the fairies gasped.

CHAPTER THIRTEEN

Wearing out the hot-pink shag rug in her bedroom suite, Raina paced back and forth. Emotions high, her mind going wild with images full of what could be happening on the human's planet. While her worries focused on the well-being of her sisters, she couldn't help but worry for Sarkis, too. *Would they kill him? Would they tell her when they returned?* Walking to a set of French doors leading out to her balcony, she pushed them open and stepped out. Scanning the whole west side of the fortress, she gazed out among the gardens at the beautiful rows of tulips encircling a granite stone water fountain.

A gigantic Koi fish made of the same stone spouted water from its thick chiseled lips. A humming bird buzzed past her head and she watched as it drew from one of three feeders she'd set on a table off to the side of her veranda. She smiled at its carefree nature. The birds and plant life were part of the world, thanks to her existence and mother-nature. Staring at the hummingbird made her wonder...*what if her sisters needed her?* The birds may not have the worries of prey as long as they stayed in Tulatopia, but evil certainly lurked on the other side and her sisters were now exposed to it.

The Watchers would give anything to make her kind extinct. Slapping her palms down on the concrete railing, she cursed. "Okay, that's it!" Running through her bedroom, she flung open another set of French doors leading to a hallway and raced across the fortress, passing the gardens. Coming to the portal she knew would be there, she took a deep breath, extended her wings and flew through it.

Breathless and trembling, Raina soared through the forest, dodging tree after tree till she approached the wooded area she shared with Sarkis...the area where they made love. Except, it didn't appear as when she last saw it. Black ash everywhere, not a speck of color to be found. Tears streamed down her face. *Wait.* Off in the distance, a flicker of color flashed. She couldn't make it out, it was too far. She followed the only bit of color until she caught sight of bodies clustered together. *Oh, no! It couldn't be.*

Her sisters were huddled up, enshrouded in a ball of flames, enclosing them.

She gazed all around and found no one else. *Not a soul.* "Magnolia! Jasmine! Peony! Freesia!" she cried out.

The heads of her sisters turned toward her voice, their complexions bleak and frail. "Raina! Get out of here! It's Lucifer—run!" Freesia screamed.

"I'm not leaving you!" Raina screeched. Trying to hold back tears, glad she followed her instincts. She tried to put out the fires with her powers, but her spell didn't work on the blazing flames. A stronger force lurked behind this. Jolting around, she reached out with her mind, hoping to seek him out. *Nothing.* From nowhere she heard a voice, a familiar voice and the words broke her heart.

"All eyes are on you my sweet. Come and see to the fate of your death."

How could she have been so stupid? She knew it was too good to be true. Demons never changed, he tricked her and won. Capturing her sisters and now her—or would he? If destiny chose this day to end her and her sisters, she came ready to put up one hell of a fight. "Come and get me, Sarkis!"

CHAPTER FOURTEEN

The scent of another fairy approached. Sarkis' master already captured four and they were getting weaker and weaker by the second. A few more minutes and they would be totally powerless for him to make his kill.

Lucifer watching from the shadows, demanded Sarkis the one to end their lives and he was all too happy to do it.

The arriving female scurried toward the others.

Sarkis watched as she attempted to put out the flames, to no avail. Grinning at her failure, his demon twitched. Taking a few steps forward, it took him a moment to draw in her features. Striking images resembling a female— close to him? *Almost if not exactly like— who?* Shaking his head, he stepped back behind a shady tree, luckily the sun caught in the clouds, granting him and his fiends enough cover to hide the best they could. Calling out to the fairy, he hoped to scare her.

Strangely, this one stood her ground, even more courageously than the others.

Wait! The sound of her voice as she shouted to the other fairies caused his head to spin—then as she called him by his name, his demon squealed in pain. Sarkis palmed his forehead; the spell Lucifer placed on him broke and in a blast of a second, he recalled everything.

Oh, gods no! Looking around, he skimmed over the remnants of the place he shared with Raina. *Ruined* and all his doing. It broke Sarkis' heart when he caught a glimpse of the look on Raina's face the second she spotted him. He turned his attention to the group of fairies trapped within the ring of fire by his master. Everything hit him like a bolt of lightning. Where he stood and what he'd done. *Nooooo.* Jerking his attention back to Raina, a sickening and disgusting expression reeked from her.

Apparently, she could not have known he wasn't in his right mind. How could he make it right? Flames closed in on the fairies and he watched as Raina remained close to them, crouching down and mumbling something, even he could not make out with his keen hearing. Hell, he couldn't concentrate on anything at the moment. Too overwhelmed at the chaos he'd caused and his own shame running through him.

The fairies' faces conveyed complete terror. Especially Raina, desperately trying to save her kind from his wrath, he knew she would be unsuccessful. Suddenly, the flames exhausted and Raina ran across the burnt marking on the ground and hugged them.

Knowing what still remained around them, he screamed out her name.

Just as he feared, Raina fell down on all fours, gasping for breath. The Witch Hazel still in full bloom caught her by surprise. The other fairies didn't even have the chance to warn her. Directing his attention over to his master, who'd been watching as well, Lucifer stalked toward them. *Do something!* His fists clinched, his eyes burned, he gritted his teeth so tight he expected them to shatter from the force.

Stepping from behind a blackened bark of wood that was once an oak, he growled, "Take one more step toward her and die!" Sarkis made his decision.

No one, not even Lucifer would harm her. Unexpectedly, his mammoth set of wings exploded from behind him, soaring tall and flapping in anger. The demon inside him wanted in on this and he willingly accepted. He'd needed the demon's aid in this fight, no doubt.

"You dare defy me?" his master retorted, glaring over his shoulder at Sarkis as he landed a few feet behind him.

"I mean it, take one more step toward them and—"

"And you will WHAT? Defeat me?" Lucifer burst into laughter, turning to face Sarkis entirely.

"You underestimate me...master. Come...if you feel I'm of no threat, what are you waiting for?" Sarkis sneered, the side of his upper lip rose in a smart-ass grin.

In a blur of a second, Lucifer flew toward the fairies and took Raina by the neck. Lifting her up, dangling her small slender limbs high above his six foot eight frame.

Sarkis' breath caught while watching her choke and gasp as her small fragile fingers desperately yanked to get free from Lucifer's grip.

"You dare come to the aid of this fucking creature? I can snap her neck with one squeeze of my hand!" Lucifer threatened.

Never uttering a word, Sarkis moved with great speed. One moment, he stood a few feet away from Lucifer and Raina, the next he had Lucifer in the same hold, held on Raina seconds before. Squeezing for dear life, his vision became replaced with a wrath he'd never known before.

No longer viewing anything around him in their normal manner, for all he saw now was red. Evil consumed him. One hand stretched out clutching his master's neck while tears ran down his face. Catching a whiff of the metallic moisture running along his skin, he realized only this type of frenzy made a demon cry blood.

The look on Lucifer's face confirmed it.

Although, Sarkis knew he could never defeat the king of darkness, he sure as hell could make this one long and damaging battle for him. Sensing his master's temperament ease, he lowered him to the ground. However, his hold remained tight. "You will no longer bring harm to those of the fairy world, do you hear me?" Sarkis shouted in a commanding voice.

"This is not over, Sarkis!" Lucifer growled under his breath.

"Today it is! And should I sense you or any fiend coming near any of them again, you will see my fury come down on you once more. I will never stop!"

"Nor will I, so be warned."

"Consider me warned, but don't forget. You have seen the power I possess. I know you're peerless, but I think you know...Even you will find it difficult to kill me. Yet, test me and I shall like to take you up on that challenge."

Lucifer's only response came in a disgusted growl.

Sarkis took that as his answer and released him.

The second his fingers parted from his master's flesh, he was struck and struck hard. Lucifer's first blow came quick. Razor sharp blades from his master's hand came down across his chest, digging deep and piercing his heart. A second blow came at his face and neck. The moment the strikes hit, Sarkis dropped onto his knees.

Lucifer knelt beside Sarkis and whispered in his ear, a smirk spreading across his hardened lips, "I warned you boy, if you play games with me, it will end with your life."

With a final push of Lucifer's finger, Sarkis collapsed to the charred ground like a rock.

Lucifer and his fiends then vanished.

CHAPTER FIFTEEN

Aiding her sisters while catching her breath from Lucifer's attack, Raina couldn't understand why Sarkis defended her. More so than when he stood against the other demon she ended up destroying earlier. The fury in his eyes and the manner of his stature almost frightened her, especially when tears of blood streamed down his face. Yet, he kept his attention directed exclusively on Lucifer. Her heart began repairing itself hearing his words of securing her race. He really did love her. It was still there, had to be.

Then Sarkis lowered Lucifer, as though hoping this would soon be all over. However, that was not the result.

Slapping her hand over her mouth to hold back the sound, she screamed at the top of her lungs when two deep slashes cut into his body. Still

screaming, she nearly fainted observing
the aftermath of the injuries as Sarkis'
limp body hit the ground with a
sickening thud, no thanks to the evil
bastard of his master.

No movement came once his body
lay prone.

Rushing to his side without pause,
she collapsed onto her knees and flipped
him onto his back. Beads of moisture
welled in her eyes as his stillness
confirmed the worst. Dead—he—was...

"Leave him, Raina, There is nothing
you can do for him. He is gone,"
Freesia's kind voice spoke behind her.

"Go! If you wish to abandon him,
the one who SAVED you, then go. I'm
staying! She leaned in, towering
protectively over his body."

"DO. AS. YOU. ARE. TOLD!"
Freesia's voice commanded.

Shedding more tears, droplets fell
on his blood-covered face and Raina
placed her hand against his blood
soaked chest, resting it over his ruined
heart. She then covered her own heart
with her other palm and cried, "I love
you. Life will never be the same because
I cannot share it with you. I'll mourn
you forever. Do you hear me? I love you
and you will always be with me." Her

sister's hand came down on her shoulder and Raina jerked away from her touch as if it burned. "I'm coming!" Standing, she didn't look at her sisters. Raina took off toward the portal.

Her sisters, Jasmine, Peony and Magnolia trailed behind her. No one spoke.

Lifting herself to sit up in bed, Raina pulled back her hot-pink fur comforter, and peeled away the white silk sheets. It took everything she possessed to try and get out of bed. *Wasn't gonna happen.* Images of Sarkis' dead body kept her from getting any sleep as she cried most of the time. Hell, she'd be crying now if she had anymore tears left. Falling back into bed, she yanked the sheet and covers back over her, pulling them over her head. She wept dry tears, wailing, "Why did you have to take him—I loved him." She cried out to no one in particular, punching her fist into the fabric.

"Well, it's nice to hear you do love me," a voice cooed from somewhere inside her room.

She again, threw back the sheets and comforter.

There standing beside her bed like a vision was Sarkis.

"What? How—Oh, by the gods! You're alive!" Raina sprang up and bounced across the mattress and jumped into Sarkis' waiting arms.

"Yes. Alive and well! I've desired to do this all day—or morning. Hell, I don't know what time it is since your world never gets dark." Sarkis laughed and sealed their mouths together in a kiss.

Despite not wanting to let go after thinking she'd lost him forever, Raina slowly pulled away. "How—how did you...?"

Sarkis gently lowered her from his arms back onto her bed. He pulled off his white t-shirt hastily and began to undo his pants.

Raina's eyes widened and her body heated with eagerness.

"Your sister, but that's all I'm going to say. Now you better have those pajamas off in the next two seconds or I'll march right back and tell her to send me—"

Raina didn't give him the chance to finish. Her silk white tank-top with pink lips came off, followed by her matching set of boy-shorts. The only thing left was a hot-pink lace thong.

"Will you do the honors my love?" Raina winked and crooked a finger for him to come to her.

He instantly felt sexual intensity in his gut. Only she managed to bring this out in him. Stepping out of his pants, he wiggled his eyebrows as Raina's eyes widened when she discovered he went commando and his cock sprung to life. One knee at a time, he crawled to her, his eyes heavy on her already aroused nipples. Oh, how she looked ready for him and he couldn't wait to find out if her treasured spot was in accordance. "Spread your legs for me," he demanded.

She obeyed.

"Now lift your arms over your head and don't move."

Raina did as instructed while she slowly and erotically outlined her lower and then upper lips with her tongue.

Sarkis almost came while he watched her tongue play. Releasing a deep inner growl he purred, "Damn woman, you turn me the fuck on!" Forgetting the idea he originally planned, Sarkis took Raina by the waist and flipped her on her stomach, swiftly lifting her ass and spreading her legs open. His massive form leaned over her with one hand supporting his weight, the other cupping her breast, and he shoved his cock deep inside her all the way to the hilt. He marveled at how tight and perfect she felt.

"More—I need more," she cried out, her long blonde locks hanging over her face.

Sarkis moved his pelvis back and forth while power plunging his cock in and out of her soaking wet canal.

"Faster, oh, I need you—faster!"

Putting his weight on his legs, he took hold of her shoulder with one hand, his other at her waist, and increased his thrusts. His driving force of greedy passion took over. The demon still contained in him smiled and took over the passionate dance. The momentum of his thrust's rapidity amplified and moans ruptured from Raina. He didn't stop until they came together.

Spinning her onto her back, he lowered his body to hers and captured her mouth. Sucking on her lips, he joined their tongues in a wrestling match and enjoyed it immensely. She still tasted like cherries, easily becoming his favorite fruit.

"Let me see them," Raina asked against his lips, taking him off guard.

"See what?" he inched his head back, so he could see the expression on her face.

"Your wings. Please? They are beautiful and a part of you. I want to see them."

It took him a moment to consider her request...But, he would deny her nothing. With one simple thought, his wings appeared and stretched out behind him. His demon purred, *See, she loves me, too.* Sarkis coughed to cover his spontaneous laughter.

When his demon wings extended fully, Raina and Sarkis laughed in unison while the ungodly span seemed to knock over everything in their path, reaching almost to the sides of the room.

"Yep. Just like I remember...Magnificent! Now make love to me again...my demon!"

Oh, how he loved the sound of that. Sarkis grinned as wide as his face would allow and at the same time, his shaft hardened, ready for round two. The softness of his wing's feathers swooped at Raina's sides in an impassioned embrace, ready to introduce her to what he had in store for her next.

Two days later...

Knocking on her sister's office door, Raina entered when she heard her sister's answering approval. She should have come to see her earlier, but Sarkis had her under lock and key for two solid days since his arrival at the fortress. "I uh, just came by to say thank you." Biting her lower lip, she actually didn't have the words to show her how thankful she truly felt at what her sister had done.

Freesia laid her pen down, scooted back from white chair painted with red tulips, and stood. Walking around her desk toward her, she halted.

Raina waited to be addressed. No words would do justice at this moment. Gazing down at the plush red rug positioned in the center of green carpet, Raina thought to herself how she would never understand her sister's taste.

"Look at me dear..."

Raina slowly lifted her eyes to meet hers.

Freesia was smiling. "You know, out of all of us, I never would have thought you'd come to surpass the others. Yet, over the past couple of days, you have surprised me, Raina. You have shown strength, honor, and courage." Freesia wrapped her arms around her and embraced her.

Raina instantly reciprocated the gesture. Squeezing a little tighter than she probably should have.

"Yes, I get it darling. You're welcome." Freesia laughed and pulled back gently. "Just know I only did it for one reason. The love you have for this male is one I have never known, never seen. It is a gift, my dear sister. I couldn't let it die. Yet, you must know something very important." Freesia headed back to her desk and sat. "He can never leave Tulatopia. If he does, he will die."

"Does he know?"

"Yes. I have explained everything to him. You know, this male of yours would do anything to keep you near." She snorted. "Hell, he almost made me blush just hearing him express the love he has for you. He simply wouldn't shut up." She rolled her eyes. "So, yes...he understands all that is necessary."

Wiping away a tear, Raina cleared her throat. "You know I'll never be able to repay what you have done. Nothing can top the love and kind—"

"My dear sister, seeing the look on your face as I do now is reward enough." She took hold of a stack of papers and arched a brow. "Now, if you don't mind, enough of the mushy-stuff. Go and begin your journey with him."

Raina giggled and turned toward the door to leave.

"Oh ah, sweetie... one more thing." Her sister pointed her white daisy tipped pen at her. "Tomorrow, continue with the spring coloration. And this time, take Gwendolyn with you. I think she's earned it."

Raina smiled and nodded. "Yes, ma'am. She'll be all too happy to hear the news!"

Heading down the hallway of the fortress, she opened the doorway leading to the gardens to find Gwendolyn smelling a new hybrid of roses Raina created when she thought she'd lost Sarkis forever. Black and pink petals signified the bond of Sarkis and Raina's love. She named them Dust of Darkness. Gwendolyn caught sight of Raina and skipped to her, wrapping her arms around her waist when finally reaching her.

"I have some good news for you. Guess who I'm taking with me tomorrow to finish this year's spring coloration?"

Gwendolyn's eyes beamed with joy squeezing tighter around Raina's waist and giggled, seeming to be electrified by the news.

Raina smiled and bent down to hug her in return and caught a glimpse of Sarkis coming from the fortress. Things were good. Spring seemed to be back on track, her sisters were back at being...well, *her sisters* and her future was now walking toward her. Life didn't get better than this.

ABOUT THE AUTHOR

Scarlet Hunter by day, works full time as a Director for a TPA (Third Party Administrator) company for Section 125 benefit plans. Residing in the outskirts of Memphis, Tennessee, when not working at her full-time job, she is found typing away on her laptop. Scarlet released her first self-publication in February 2013 with Curator's Curse, Book One of Legends of the Immortal Bloods Series. As an avid reader, Scarlet's love of science-fiction/paranormal romances inspired her to pursue her dream of writing. You can visit her at www.scarlethunter.com to find all the great stuff in the works.

Web Links:

Website: www.scarlethunter.com
Blog:
http://scarlethunter11.blogspot.com
/
Facebook Fan Page:
http://www.facebook.com/ScarletHu
nter11
Facebook page:
http://www.facebook.com/ScarletHu
nter
Amazon author page:
http://www.amazon.com/Scarlet-
Hunter/e/B007JB97JI/ref=sr_tc_2_0?
qid=1346698720&sr=1-2-ent

OTHER BOOKS BY SCARLET HUNTER

Curator's Curse, Book One, Legends of the Immortal Bloods

Coming In 2014

-Thirst of the Sea
-Snowline's Visitor, Book One, Arise of the Guardians
-Heaven's Sacrifice
-Burning Salvation
-Blood Eternal, Book Two, Legends of the Immortal Bloods

Coming 2015

-Mid-Night Mountain, Book Two, Arise of the Guardians

-Demon's Light, Book Two, The Reign of Darkness

Scarlet Hunter, Author
www.scarlethunter.com